I Wanna Iguana

KAREN KAUFMAN ORLOFF • ILLUSTRATED BY DAVID CATROW

SCHOLASTIC INC.

New York   Toronto   London   Auckland   Sydney
Mexico City   New Delhi   Hong Kong   Buenos Aires

D0521598

ISBN 0-439-80015-3

Text copyright © 2004 by Karen Kaufman Orloff.
Illustrations copyright © 2004 by David Catrow. All rights reserved.
Published by Scholastic Inc., 557 Broadway, New York, NY 10012, by arrangement with G. P. Putnam's Sons, an imprint of Penguin Putnam Books for Young Readers, a division of Penguin Group (USA) Inc. SCHOLASTIC and associated logos are trademarks and/or registered trademarks of Scholastic Inc.

12 11 10 9 8 7 6 5   7 8 9 10/0

Printed in the U.S.A.   40

First Scholastic printing, September 2005

Designed by Marikka Tamura. Text set in Catchup and Comic Sans.
The art was done in pencil and watercolor.

To Max and Emily
for their inspiration,
to Brad for his support,
and to all my writer friends
for making me work harder. —K.K.O.

To Mr. Alexander—
you taught me discipline
and how to be an artist. —D.C.

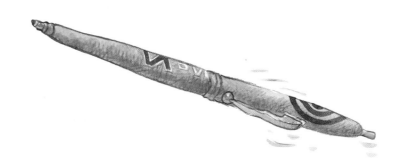

Dear Mom,

I know you don't think I should have Mikey Gulligan's baby iguana when he moves, but here's why I should.

If I don't take it, he goes to Stinky and Stinky's dog, Lurch, will eat it. You don't want that to happen, do you?

Signed,
Your sensitive son,
Alex

Dear Alex,
I'm glad you're so compassionate,
but I doubt that Stinky's mother
will let Lurch get into
the iguana's cage.
Nice try, though.

Love,
Mom

Dear Alex,
Tarantulas are quiet too, but I wouldn't want one as a pet. By the way, that iguana of Mikey's is uglier than Godzilla. Just thought I'd mention it.

Love,
Mom

Dear Mom,
You would never even have to see the iguana. I'll keep his cage in my room on the dresser next to my soccer trophies. Plus, he's so small, I bet you'll never even know he's there.
Love and a zillion and one kisses,
Alex

Dear Alex,

How are you going to get a girl to marry you when you own a six-foot-long reptile?

Love,

Your concerned mother

This iguana can be the brother I've always wanted.
Love,
Your lonely child, Alex

Dear Mom,
I know I have a brother but he's just a baby. What fun is that? If I had an iguana, I could teach it tricks and things.
Ethan doesn't do tricks.
He just burps and poops.
Love,
Grossed-out Alex

Dear Mom,

If I knew the fish was going to
jump into the spaghetti sauce,
I never would have taken
the cover off the jar!

Love,
Your son who has
learned his lesson

P.S. Iguanas don't like spaghetti.

Dear Alex,
A trial basis means Dad and I see how well you take care of him for a week or two before we decide if you can have him forever. Remember, Stinky and Lurch are waiting!
Love,
Mom

P.S. If you clean his cage as well as you clean your room, you're in trouble.

"Are you sure you want to do this, Alex?"

"Yes, Mom!
I wanna iguana....
Please!"

Dear Alex,

Look on your dresser.

Love,

Mom